DECIDE YOUR DESTINY

BBC CHILDREN'S BOOKS
Published by the Penguin Group
Penguin Books Ltd, 80 Strand, London, WC2R 0RL, England
Penguin Group (USA) Inc., 375 Hudson Street, New York, New York 10014, USA
Penguin Books (Australia) Ltd, 250 Camberwell Road, Camberwell, Victoria 3124, Australia
(A division of Pearson Australia Group Pty Ltd)
Canada, India, New Zealand, South Africa
Published by BBC Children's Books, 2007
This edition produced for The Book People Ltd, Hall Wood Avenue, Haydock, St Helens. WA11 9UL.
Text and design © Children's Character Books, 2007
Written by Richard Dungworth
10 9 8 7 6 5 4 3 2 1
BBC and logo © and TM BBC 1996. Doctor Who logo © BBC 2004. TARDIS image © BBC 1963.
Dalek image © BBC/Terry Nation 1963. Licensed by BBC Worldwide Limited.
DOCTOR WHO, TARDIS and DALEK and the DOCTOR WHO, TARDIS and DALEK logos are
trade marks of the British Broadcasting Corporation and are used under licence.
ISBN-13: 978-1-85613-149-0
ISBN-10: 1-85613-149-1
Printed in Great Britain by Clays Ltd, St Ives plc

DOCTOR·WHO

DECIDE YOUR DESTINY

Second Skin

by Richard Dungworth

Second Skin

1 You're strolling to the corner shop, when a loud clang behind you causes you to turn in alarm.

A manhole cover lies upturned in the centre of the road. A man in a pinstriped suit is hauling himself backwards through the manhole, eyes fixed on the depths below. He is holding a slim silver torch in one hand, keeping its blue beam trained on something out of sight. As he gets to his feet, he gives you an exasperated look.

'Sewers! Why is it always sewers?'

As he gradually elevates his peculiar torch, you catch your first glimpse of the beam's target. Four metres from its source, the blue light splits into a network of thinner beams, which enclose a glistening, indigo-coloured mass. It is the size of a beach ball, and looks like a knot of giant eels, unnaturally compressed into a writhing, rubbery clump.

'I mean, is it compulsory to lurk in smelly underground tunnels? Is it in the Universal Rulebook of Lurking, or something?'

The stranger continues to elevate the beam, and the unpleasant gristly thing at its tip emerges fully from the manhole.

'I'd like to think that if I'd travelled across several galaxies to feast upon another life form, I'd at least try to hang out somewhere a bit less dreary. Somewhere on the Mediterranean coast, perhaps. But no — it's always sewers! Here, hold this for a second.'

Before you can object, the man has thrust the silver torch into your hand.

'Sonic screwdriver. Just keep the beam trained on the ugly squishy thing. That's it — lovely! I just need to grab a Containment Cell from the TARDIS. Back in a mo.'

And he hurriedly crosses to where a large blue box, with POLICE PUBLIC CALL BOX above its double doors, stands on the opposite pavement. Although you've never noticed it there before…

As the stranger disappears inside the blue box, you're left staring incredulously at the squirming sphere, hovering only a few metres away.

Suddenly, the device in your hand throws off a shower of sparks. Its beam fizzles momentarily, then dies altogether.

The net constraining it disappears and the strange purple clump expands explosively, in a sickening squelch of uncoiling, wet flesh. You find yourself confronted with a monstrous creature, over ten metres across. Its dozen sinuous arms surround a drooling maw, lined with multiple rows of cruel curved teeth.

You stagger backwards in terror and the monster rears up, clearly preparing to strike, and lets out a blood-curdling shriek.

The man in the pinstriped suit bursts from the blue box's doors.

'Quick — get inside!'

To do as the stranger says, and enter the box, go to 32. To make a run for it along the street, go to 14.

2 The Shiner passes, and continues on his patrol. As he moves away, the Doctor gestures to the group escorting the fuel cells.

'If we can stop them loading those cells, she'll not be able to take off. I think it's time we gave them a bit of a shock...'

Taking the Doctor's hint, you grasp the antidote device firmly. As he breaks from cover, sonic in hand, you accompany him, dashing for the fuel cell cart. As you approach, you unleash a series of crackling white flares from the device. Three of the Shiners go down. But when you squeeze the trigger again, nothing happens. You're out of charge.

The remaining Shiners quickly return your fire, and you're driven back. As you retreat, the Doctor points to the small spacecraft nearby.

'Maybe that patrol ship has some firepower we could use!'

To head for the patrol ship, go to 37. To try to find cover, go to 24.

3 You remember the Doctor's anti-sickness tip as you hurriedly follow him into the Zoob. As a result, you feel more or less okay as you step out into a different Apex a split second later.

Before you can take in your new surroundings, the Doctor pulls you down behind a large cabinet. As you peer cautiously around it, you see why.

The entire area — a laboratory of some kind — is bustling with humanoid figures. At first glance, you take them for ordinary human beings. But there is something distinctly odd about them. Their skin, wherever it is exposed, has a peculiar sheen — almost as if it were shimmering. And there is something very wrong with their eyes. They are metallic silver, without iris or pupil.

These inhuman humanoids are overseeing the automated packing of three large white pods that stand at the centre of the laboratory. Under their silent direction, robotic loaders are gathering cylindrical canisters from the laboratory's hi-tech workstations, and slotting each one neatly into a snug housing within one of the pods.

The Doctor nudges you, and gestures to the far side of the laboratory, where a doorway stands open.

To sneak around to the lab's exit, under cover of the workstations, go to 38. To keep watching from where you are, go to 44.

4 As you try desperately to pull one of the Shiners off the Doctor, it flings you away. You crack your head against the TARDIS, and black out.

The next thing you notice is a chill against your back. Your T-shirt has been removed, and you appear to be pinned down against a cold, metallic surface.

The strange device hovering over you slowly comes into focus. It's a robotic arm. Its claw-like manipulator holds a small translucent patch, which it is lining up with the top of your sternum.

There is a loud clang, and the robotic arm topples sideways. Blip is suddenly leaning over you, holding a thick metal bar.

'Let's get you out of here!'

He releases the restraints around your wrists and ankles, grabs the tissue patch, and hurriedly helps you to the room's exit. Just along the corridor outside is the opening of a Zoob. You can hear approaching footsteps.

'Shiners!' hisses Blip.

To dash for the Zoob, go to 11. To duck back inside the grafting theatre and find somewhere to hide, go to 69.

5 'Not both of them!' yells the Doctor – but too late.

You're flung sideways as the floor suddenly shifts. A rushing sound, rising and falling in volume, fills your head as the entire area around you becomes a lurching, shaking chaos. Then, as abruptly as the maelstrom started, it stops.

Your companion releases his anxious grip on the control console, blowing out his cheeks.

'I was only planning a small spatial jump – just to get us clear,' he says. 'But that second lever you yanked activates the Augmentation Loop. Sort of emergency booster. It's magnified our movement a fair bit – according to my readouts, we've jumped over 200 years.'

You look at him uncomprehendingly.

'The TARDIS.' The stranger gestures to your surroundings. 'It's a machine for travelling in space and time.'

'Rrrright.' He's clearly bonkers. 'And that would make you…?'

'A Time Lord,' beams your companion. 'Last one. You can call me the Doctor.' He claps his hands purposefully. 'Now – let's see where you've landed us!'

> To tell the stranger that you think he's lost his marbles, go to 81. To head back outside through the doors, go to 29.

6 **A**n instant after you step into the Zoob, you stagger from its fluorescent glare to find yourself in one corner of a vast, vault-like chamber — a giant hangar. At the sound of activity nearby, you and the Doctor quickly take cover behind a stack of containers.

In the centre of the hangar floor squats a massive barrel-shaped spacecraft. Its glossy hull bears the name Fat Lady. Cargo doors in the ship's starboard side stand open, allowing a steady flow of large white cargo pods to enter its hold. The pods hover magically above a gravity-negating conveyor, floating smoothly along the conveyor's length from where it enters the hangar through an opening in the wall near where you are crouching.

'Packed with Second Skin patches,' whispers the Doctor.

All around the huge craft, a mixed host of Shiners and service drones are bustling about, overseeing the loading procedure and running pre-launch checks.

'We've got to stop her taking off. If we can get inside, I might be able to sabotage the flight systems.'

The Doctor points to where a group of Shiners are escorting a pair of distinctive black-and-gold robots, on a hover-trolley, towards a circular hatch near the front of the Fat Lady's hull.

'Or we could just try to take out those two. They're cosmobots. Operate the flight systems on orbital freighters like this one. If we can stop them boarding, she'll be going nowhere...'

To ambush the cosmobot group, go to 63. To sneak across to the anti-gravity conveyor and clamber on top of a moving cargo pod, to hitch a ride into the ship's interior, go to 25

7 | Your efforts are in vain, and your capture by the hostile silver-eyed creatures seems inevitable.

Then suddenly, a pinpoint of light appears in the nearby wall, rapidly expanding into the luminous opening of a Zoob. A small boy, not more than nine years old, steps out of it. He is striking in appearance — white-haired, with very fair skin and a purplish tint to his pale eyes.

'Quick! In here!'

You dive for the Zoob entrance, and are sucked powerfully forward, then spat out into entirely different surroundings — an empty storeroom. The Doctor emerges immediately after you, then the boy, who seals the Zoob behind him.

'This way!'

The child hurries to the centre of the room, kneels, and with a well-rehearsed slap, releases a loose panel in the floor. Beneath it is a secret space, not more than a few cubic metres in size. It is littered with blankets, food wrappers, electronic bits and bobs, and other miscellaneous junk.

The three of you drop down into the cramped den, and the boy quickly pulls the floor panel back into place. He flops down onto a blanket and grabs a bottle of thick blue liquid from among the junk. After thirstily swallowing a few mouthfuls, he offers the bottle to you.

To take a swig, go to 34. To say you're not thirsty, thanks, go to 71.

Following the Doctor's advice, you shut your eyes tightly. Nevertheless, travelling by Zoob proves rather unpleasant — a burst of acceleration and an equally extreme braking force, compressed into a brief, disorientating jolt.

You stumble out into an entirely new location. Moments later, the Doctor emerges from the Zoob's green glow, looking as wobbly as you feel.

'Oooo! Perhaps it's your ears you're supposed to close…'

The Zoob has brought you to one end of the central aisle of a large warehouse, lined with rows of racking. A corridor leads from the far end of the aisle. The shelves on either side of you are stacked with a variety of containers, mostly white, all bearing a red SKINTHETIC logo. The Doctor scans the labels of those nearest you.

'Laser scalpels…pre-op sterile wipes…saline solution — someone round here likes their surgical equipment.'

To search for further clues as to what exactly the Skinthetic company does, go to 94. To head for the corridor, go to 60.

9 After a short distance, the corridor turns sharply to the left. As you round the corner, you unintentionally catch up with the silver-eyed humanoid that the Doctor brainwashed minutes earlier. It is operating a console in the wall a few metres further along the corridor.

At your sudden appearance, the creature turns from the console to direct its eerie gaze at you and the Doctor.

'There is no data-match for a Ministry of Viral Control.'

'Ah,' replies the Doctor. 'Well…that's because it's a top-secret department, obviously. Very hush-hush.'

'You are intruders.' The creature's voice is emotionless. 'You must be grafted. All humans must be grafted.'

As you hear the echo of multiple footsteps further along the corridor, you realise that the humanoid hasn't only been using the control screen to check out the Doctor's story. Reinforcements are clearly on their way.

To stand your ground, go to 55. To run for your life, go to 83.

10 You fire a charge from the antidote device. As it hits the Shiner in the chest, its silver eyes widen momentarily in shock, then it slumps to the floor.

You and the Doctor hurriedly drag the body to the wall, out of view. Two gigantic machines stand nearby, each nearly twice the height of a man, with heavy mechanical limbs. The torso of each machine incorporates a harness and control panel — clearly meant to accommodate a human operator.

'Robo-loaders,' says the Doctor. 'For handling heavy stuff. Those fists could do some real damage. Maybe enough to put the Fat Lady out of action…'

He clambers up into the first machine, secures its harness, and grasps the twin control levers. With a hiss and clunk, the metal giant takes a heavy stride away from the wall.

'Wait here!' the Doctor shouts, as he stomps off in the robo-loader, heading for the Fat Lady.

To do as the Doctor asks, and stay back, go to 43. To have a go at piloting the second loader, go to 73.

The Zoob takes you to a room filled with hi-tech communications equipment. Blip quickly moves to the nearest display console.

'Maybe some of the recent transmissions back to Earth might help us make some sense of what's been happening.'

He scans an on-screen list.

'That's odd — the last message never got sent. Let's have a look...'

As he touches the screen, a 3-D projection of a man's face appears above the console. He begins speaking very rapidly, clearly in a state of panic.

'This is Professor Treffin, chief scientist on the Skinthetic orbiting platform. This is an urgent transmission for Earthport Nine. A ship is being prepared for departure from this facility at 1500 hours. I am powerless to prevent its launch, but it must not, I repeat must not be permitted to land. The vessel is carrying a shipment of 50 million Second Skin patches, for global distribution. This must be prevented at all costs. There is a — '

You hear footsteps in the background, the Professor's eyes widen in fear, and the transmission cuts out.

'Guess the Shiners got him,' says Blip. 'Still doesn't tell us why the patches make you change.'

'They're alien.'

The Doctor is standing in a doorway at the other side of the room, a peculiar device slung across his back.

'Each patch is a colony of exo-parasites — lifeforms which survive by encapsulating a host, then hijacking its biological systems. Treffin didn't manufacture a synthetic skin, like he claimed. He discovered a patch of existing tissue that was UV-resistant, and saw the commercial potential. Probably picked it up at a meteorite strike site. Didn't realise what he'd found was actually a parasitic alien lifeform. That's what all the Second Skin patches are cloned from.'

'And millions of them are about to be sent to Earth?'

'Not if I can help it,' replies the Doctor. 'Blip, I want you to see if you can get that transmission through to Earthport Nine. We'll head for the hangar, and see if it isn't too late to stop the launch.'

You hurry after the Doctor as he leads you quickly along a corridor, then halts in front of a glowing Zoob entrance.

'If I'm right, this should take us to Capricorn Apex — the main hangar.'

To ask the Doctor what he's planning once you get there, go to 23. To ask what the device he's carrying is, go to 77.

Several of the advancing Shiners have now drawn weapons. As a volley of laser bolts comes fizzing your way, the Doctor drags you out of the line of fire.

'It's no good! There are too many of them!'

Hastily retreating, you hear a crackling roar behind you. The Fat Lady is beginning to lift off. Glancing over your shoulder, you see her making for the hangar exit, held aloft by powerful rockets under her wide belly.

As you dash through one of the hangar's exits, the Doctor thrusts his sonic screwdriver against its control panel. A shower of sparks erupts from the panel and the door slices shut behind you. You hear several bodies slam against it.

Through a window in the passageway you've entered you can see the Fat Lady, now space-bound, moving slowly away from the hangar mouth. As he watches her, the Doctor's expression is sombre.

'If only we could shoot her down — but this station's unarmed.'

'All those pods...' you murmur, horrified by the threat to humankind posed by the ship's sinister cargo.

The Doctor's face suddenly lights up.

'Pods! That's it! You're a genius!'

Without further explanation, he sprints along the passageway to where a small hexagonal hatch is located beside another window. It is marked EMERGENCY ACCESS ONLY. You've seen similar hatches elsewhere.

The Doctor quickly opens the hatch, revealing a small chamber beyond.

'Emergency escape pod,' explains the Doctor, prising a panel from the pod's interior and applying his sonic screwdriver. 'If I reset its launch thrusters for a single powerful burst, we've got ourselves a makeshift missile.'

He slams the panel shut and reseals the hatch. Through the window, you can see the Fat Lady, now moving parallel to the passageway you're in. The Doctor's hand hovers over a glowing red button.

'Just a bit further...NOW!'

He hits the button, and the escape pod's thrusters roar into life. The pod rockets away from the space station, hurtling a hundred metres across space — straight into the Fat Lady's side. The vast ship is instantaneously engulfed in a giant ball of flames.

'YES!'

You punch the air, sharing the Doctor's delight.

'Right!' beams the Doctor. 'We'd best track down young Blip and sort out a couple more antidote guns for the pair of you. Shouldn't take us too long to decontaminate the rest of our Shiner friends.'

He puts his arm around your shoulder.

'After that, how do you fancy a quick tour of twenty-third century Earth? I've got time on my hands, as it happens...'

THE END

13 | The Doctor strides boldly forward to meet the approaching humanoid, holding up his blank sheet of psychic paper.

'Agents Milton and Wordsworth, Ministry of Viral Control. Don't come any closer! Your associate here is highly contagious.'

The creature halts, and fixes its silver-eyed stare on the paper, clearly puzzled. The Doctor presses on, improvising brilliantly.

'I'm afraid you've got a Class Two Retrovirus on board. Looks like the T5 strain. Nasty stuff. We're going to need a full Medi-Kit and Isolation Tent as quickly as possible, please.'

The humanoid hesitates momentarily, then turns and hurries away.

The Doctor gives you a cheeky wink, and slips the paper back into his pocket.

'Now — let's get out of here, before our charming patient wakes up...'

To wait a few moments, then set off in the same direction as the humanoid, go to 9.
To head the opposite way, go to 38.

You don't get far. There's a swishing noise behind you, and a slimy tentacle coils around your ankle. You find yourself being dragged back towards the creature's hideous mouth.

An instant later, the beast gives another ear-splitting shriek, and releases its grip.

'Get up!'

The man in the pinstriped suit hauls you to your feet. He bundles you quickly across the road and through the doors of the blue box. You're barely aware of his next actions, as your brain struggles to take in the box's mind-bending interior. It is huge — a vast, arching cavern.

'But...'

'Uh-huh. Wacky, isn't it?' Your companion is now busily operating the buttons and levers of a control console that stands on a raised platform at the centre of this impossible space.

'We need to get out of here sharpish. Miss Lovelylooks out there dropped you because I spiked her with a Time Mine. When it goes off — in about thirty seconds — it'll radiate a displacement field the size of a tennis court, translating anything non-terrestrial within it to a random backwater of time and space. Not a trip I particularly fancy.'

He slaps a final button, and stands back expectantly. Nothing happens. He gives the side of the console a frustrated kick.

'Arrgh! One of the Prothilium coils must have blown again.'

He spins to face you urgently.

'Quick! Try the reserve coils! The big lever by your side!'

You hesitate — there are two 'big levers' within your reach.

'We're out of time!' yells your companion. 'Pull the lever — NOW!'

To pull the left-hand lever, go to 40.
To hedge your bets, and pull both, go to 5.

Before you can take the second gadget from the Doctor, the doors at the end of the chamber slice open and you are spat out into the blackness of space.

After a few seconds of panic, you realise that your helmet is, at least, enabling you to breathe. But the space station is rapidly receding.

The Doctor, too, is drifting helplessly. But as you watch, he aims the second device back towards the space station's hull. A small, blunt-headed projectile shoots from it, unspooling a thin line. As it thuds against the side of the hull, it sticks to it.

The Doctor is now gesturing wildly to you, miming the use of the hairdryer-like device you're clutching. You squeeze its trigger experimentally, and feel yourself propelled in the opposite direction to the one in which it's pointing.

You manage to use the thruster to steer yourself over to where the Doctor is tethered. As you cling to his back, he activates the spooler on his harpoon gun, and you are reeled back to the hull of the space station.

Using the maintenance grab-rails, you should be able to make it to either of two nearby airlock hatches.

To head for the hatch marked C2, go to 79.
To opt for the other one, go to 27.

As you engage with the device's interface, your field of vision goes black, but for a flashing alert:

BIOMETRIC LOG-IN INITIATED

SCANNING RETINA

You feel a momentary hotness at the back of your eyes, then a second message replaces the first:

LOG-IN UNSUCCESSFUL

SECURITY SYSTEMS ACTIVATED

An instant later, an agonisingly bright glare floods your mind, and you know no more.

* * *

You slowly come round, to find yourself slumped over something that is jogging up and down. As your mind clears, you realise it is the Doctor's shoulder. He has you in a fireman's lift, and is hurrying along a curving corridor. At the sound of your groan, he stops to lower you onto your unsteady legs.

'Welcome back! Sorry for the undignified mode of transport, but I had to get you out of there in a hurry! When the system identified you as unauthorised personnel, it knocked you out with a neural pulse, and set off the alarms.

There were robots all over the place in seconds. Service drones, by the looks of them — cleaning, catering and repair machines. All reprogrammed to act as security. Though I can't imagine why —'

He breaks off at the sound of approaching footfalls — rapid and numerous — from around the bend ahead.

'Quick — in there!'

There is a recess in the corridor wall just ahead, housing the glowing entrance to another Zoom Tube.

To hide inside the recess, go to 62.
To escape by entering the Zoob, go to 3.

You step out of the box's narrow double doors and, to your bewilderment, find that you are no longer where you were. Instead, the TARDIS appears to be standing in the centre of a circular, silver-walled room.

There is a strange opening in one curved wall, veiled by a haze of purple light. Hovering beside this glowing opening is a hi-tech trolley, loaded with neatly-stacked white canisters. Each bears the word SKINTHETIC in red lettering.

'Aha! A clue!' says the Doctor excitedly.

He delves in his jacket pocket, and pulls out a small black cube, the size of a sugar lump. Kneeling, he places it on the floor, and presses its top surface. Each face of the cube suddenly unfolds, repeatedly, until an ultra-thin matt-black rectangle about fifty centimetres across has unfurled itself. As the Doctor touches it, the black surface instantly becomes brightly illuminated.

'Something I picked up at an end-of-millennium table-top sale,' explains the Doctor, grinning up at you. 'Encyclopaedia Britannica, Twenty-Third Edition.'

You watch as his fingers dance across the touchscreen. An instant later, it flashes up the relevant entry:

SKINTHETIC CORPORATION: Early twenty-third Earth Century bio-engineering company. Corporate headquarters and manufacturing laboratories located on the ISO-SPHERE.

The Doctor quickly selects the hyperlink:

ISO-SPHERE: Earth-orbiting experimental space-station, characterised by its structural geometry, based on an isohedron (a shape made of 20 triangular faces, with 12 apexes, approximating a sphere). Operational from Earth Year 2217 to 2226.

As the Doctor deactivates the encyclopaedia, it quickly reverts to a tiny cube.

'Well, now we know where — and when — we are, how do you fancy a look around?'

To try the glowing opening, go to 57.
To explore this area further, go to 93.

18 You hit the Fat Lady's hull hard, and scrabble to grip its smooth surface. You feel yourself sliding backwards — until the Doctor, clinging to the hull beside you, grabs your wrist. He is somehow using his sonic screwdriver to hold on.

With the Doctor's help, you haul yourself up onto the top of the massive spacecraft. But your heart sinks as you look back at the slope you've just climbed to see several Shiners rapidly ascending in pursuit.

'Looks like UV resistance isn't the only "special property" that alien skin has,' observes the Doctor. 'They grip like spiders!'

You hurry across the Fat Lady's broad back to her other flank. Together, you sit, legs extended, and push yourselves over the edge. An exhilarating slide ride takes you back down to the hangar floor.

To duck under the Fat Lady's wide belly in an attempt to evade your pursuers, go to 24. To prepare to attack them as they drop down after you, go to 12.

You hurry after Blip, dashing along a number of corridors before ducking through a doorway into a small office. As you look around, you hear an odd whimpering noise coming from behind a desk in one corner of the room. Cautiously, you investigate.

Cowering behind the desk is a middle-aged man in a lab coat. He meets your puzzled gaze with eyes wide with fear — but not silver.

'I know you,' says Blip, unexpectedly. 'You're the top Skinthetic bod, Professor thingy — the one what wanted me to have a graft.'

'It was a mistake!' replies the man, hysterically. 'The whole project is a terrible mistake! The tissue we clone the Second Skin patches from — we didn't make it. I found it, in a fragment of comet ice. Its properties were so astounding — self-replication, UV-resistance — that I realised its commercial potential immediately. I set up Skinthetic, and began working on Second Skin, using the tissue to generate cloned cells. But there must something wrong with it...'

'It's an exo-parasite.'

The Doctor has appeared in the doorway.

'Lives off other lifeforms by encapsulating them, then tapping into the nervous system. Hijacks the host's biological systems completely, assuming total control of its body.'

He gestures to a strange device slung across his back.

'I've put together an antidote — a gamma pulse, which should reboot the host's neural control. But there's only enough juice for a few charges.'

The Professor approaches the Doctor, grasping his lapels.

'It's no good! You might be able to deal with the ones on board, but that's just the tip of the iceberg! There's a ship being loaded with Second Skin patches in this facility's hangar as we speak. Millions of them, destined for Earth. They've been promoted worldwide — it'll only be a matter of days before the infection goes global!'

The Doctor pulls away urgently.

'How do we get to the hangar?'

'The corridor outside. If you follow it to the left, you'll come to a pair of Zoobs. One goes to Leo Apex — the hangar area. I forget which…'

The Doctor asks Blip to keep an eye on the distraut Professor, then rushes with you to the nearby Zoobs.

To take the left-hand Zoob, go to 6. To take the one on the right, go to 47.

A smooth black console stands against one wall. There is something spherical hovering above it. As you cross to take a closer look, you recognise it as a 3-D projection of the space station you've arrived on, with twelve Apex units held in the complex shape of an isohedron by thirty thick tubular struts.

The console displays the words ISO-SPHERE NAVIGATOR, but is otherwise featureless. There is a slim black visor lying on top of it. The Doctor picks it up and examines it.

'Some sort of neural interface. The system must be mind-operated. You probably get a virtual tour of the station.'

He looks about him, taking in the three identical corridors that stretch away from the area you're in.

'We could certainly use a little help finding our way around. On the other hand, these early mind-control interfaces are notoriously dodgy...'

To try on the visor, go to 16. To choose one of the corridors, go to 60.

Your delaying tactic works, giving you time to make your getaway. After hurrying along several corridors, the Doctor leads you through a side door, sealing it behind you.

A rhythmic hsss-plunk-tsshhh fills the room you've entered. A small white machine spits out a slim translucent wafer, the size of a credit card and falls onto a conveyor field. The Doctor takes one of the wafers from the conveyor and examines it. As he lifts it to eye-level, you are astonished to see text scrolling across its surface.

'It's a Patient Information Chip. For something called a "Second Skin Anti-UV Patch".'

He reads silently for a few moments.

'So that's what Skinthetic are all about. They've bioengineered a product to protect people from UV radiation. I'd forgotten what a big problem the sun has become by this Earth era — there's no ozone layer left to speak of, so humans are at constant risk of skin cancer. According to this, Skinthetic have developed a patch of synthetic tissue that you stick on your chest. It rapidly divides to cover your entire body in a thin UV-proof layer — a "second skin". Quite ingenious!'

You think the whole idea sounds a bit creepy. To ask the Doctor if he agrees, go to 92. To follow the conveyor out of the room, go to 46.

You shriek at the Doctor's silver-eyed assailant that there is no need to harm him, that you both submit, that you'll cooperate with whatever his demands are. But your pleading is in vain.

The Doctor is fading fast. Having given up trying to break his attacker's choking hold, he fumbles in his suit pocket and withdraws his sonic screwdriver. But as its tip flares with blue light, the Doctor finally succumbs to lack of oxygen. The screwdriver slips from his limp hand and clatters to the floor.

Without hesitation, you grab the glowing sonic screwdriver, and thrust its tip against the humanoid's arm. The creature gives a startled grunt, releases its grip on the Doctor's neck, and both he and the Doctor slump to the floor.

With great relief, you hear the Doctor take a shuddering intake of breath. Moments later, his eyes reopen — he's okay.

But your relief is short-lived. As you help the Doctor back to his feet, you see another humanoid figure approaching.

'Psychic paper,' croaks the Doctor, inexplicably. He hurriedly delves in another pocket and pulls out a blank piece of paper. 'I might be able to brainwash him with this.'

To go along with whatever the Doctor has planned, go to 13. To urge him to run for it, go to 83.

Before you can discuss a plan of action, a group of Shiners burst onto the scene, weapons drawn. Without hesitation, the Doctor slips the strange device from his shoulder, and uses it to unleash a series of crackling white flares of energy.

All four Shiners slump to the floor.

'It's okay — they're not dead!' the Doctor reassures you, seeing the horrified look on your face. 'And when they come round, they'll have regained control of their own bodies, with any luck.'

He passes you the device.

'It's my antidote for our infestation problem. Its electromagnetic charge kick-starts the human host's own nervous system, helping them overthrow the exo-parasite's control. Uses a lot of juice, though. I'd guess we've only five or six charges left, so use it wisely.'

With that, he turns and strides into the Zoob. As you follow, you experience the familiar momentary lurch, then emerge into a vast, high-ceilinged chamber. You've been transported to Capricorn Apex, the station's hangar area.

A van-sized space vehicle with stub wings and a cluster of rear rocket thrusters is parked a little distance away. But this craft is dwarfed by the looming bulk of the Fat Lady, a colossal space-freighter that squats at the centre of the hangar floor. All around her, Shiners and service drones are scurrying about.

'Look like they're running pre-launch checks,' says the Doctor. 'We need to think of something fast if we're going to stop her taking off.'

He gestures to the smaller spacecraft. 'Maybe we could use that astro-tug to ram her — damage her enough that she can't fly. Or if we could get on board somehow...'

To approach the Fat Lady, in the hope of finding a way to sneak on board, go to 68.
To head for the astro-tug, go to 37.

Despite your best efforts to evade them, the Shiners close in. It looks like the game is up.

Suddenly, a small flying vehicle bursts through their ranks, sending them sprawling. As the hover-cart sweeps to a halt in front of you, you recognise its white-haired pilot.

'Blip!'

'Get in! Quick!'

You don't need to be asked twice. As you and the Doctor pile into the back of the hover-cart, Blip swings it round and sends it speeding across the hangar.

But as you race towards one of the exits, the Doctor signals for Blip to bring the vehicle to a halt. Over the hum of its idling motor you can hear a loud klaxon. The Shiners and service drones are responding to its sound by vacating the hangar area. You understand why as an orange inferno blazes into life beneath the Fat Lady's belly. The wave of heat that hits you is overpowering.

'She's going to launch,' says the Doctor. 'I've got to stop her.'

Sure enough, the giant ship is beginning to move steadily towards the hangar doors.

'You two jump out — I've got an idea.'

You and Blip reluctantly drop to the hangar floor. You watch anxiously as the Doctor urges the hover-cart at full speed towards the Fat Lady. He is going flat out, gaining rapidly on the giant freighter as it reaches the hangar's threshold and edges out into the void beyond.

At the last moment, the Doctor leaps from the speeding cart. The tiny vehicle continues on its flight path, disappearing into one of the Fat Lady's gaping engine intakes, just as the ship clears the hangar.

For a drawn-out second or two, it seems that swallowing the hover-cart hasn't affected the engine. The Fat Lady continues to glide steadily out into space. Then, with a blinding flash and deafening boom, the engine explodes. The colossal spaceship disintegrates instantaneously, blown apart in a vast ball of flame.

You and Blip wait for the shockwave to pass, then dash across the hangar to where the Doctor is sprawled on the debris-strewn floor. As you help him to his feet, he gives you a broad grin.

'Not bad for an old man, eh?'

He brushes down his suit.

'Now then — we'd best put together a couple more antidote guns, and see if we can sort out the rest of those Shiners. After that, Blip, we'll take you home in the TARDIS. Maybe you could show me and my friend here a few twenty-third century sights?'

THE END

25 You and the Doctor flatten yourselves against the top of the floating cargo pod, hoping to avoid detection. But as the pod approaches the ship's hold, there's a yell. A moment later, its side is raked with red laser fire. You've been spotted.

'Go!' yells the Doctor, rising suddenly and unleashing a volley of charges from his antidote device. Three of the rapidly approaching group of Shiners hit the floor. But others now begin to converge on your pod, firing as they come.

There's a metre gap between each pair of floating pods. Fuelled by fear, you clear the first gap, then the second, then the third, leaping from one pod to the next as laser blasts fill the air around you. You are now only metres from the Fat Lady's mammoth belly.

To duck down again and ride the cargo pod into the Fat Lady's hold, go to 85. To evade the laser fire by leaping onto the outside of the ship's hull, go to 18.

As the Doctor struggles with the locked laboratory doors, you take a closer look at the workstations. Each one includes a small sealed unit that reminds you of a miniature hospital incubator.

Out of the corner of your eye, you notice a flare of light. The entrance to the lab's Zoob is suddenly glowing more brightly.

'Doctor!'

As you and the Doctor dive for cover, two figures step from the Zoob. Both are carrying hi-tech firearms. Separating, they move among the laboratory's rows of workstations, scanning the area with their inhuman silver eyes.

The first figure gives an impatient grunt, and moves to the doorway — passing within metres of where the Doctor is crouched in hiding. At the humanoid's command, the doors hiss open. He strides into the corridor beyond, his associate following silently.

> **To surprise the pair, in an attempt to overpower them, go to 7. To wait until they have moved off, then follow the corridor, go to 38.**

27 | The hatch hisses open, and you clamber into the airlock chamber beyond. The Doctor seals the hatch, then activates the re-pressurisation controls. As he removes his helmet, you follow suit.

'Ahh, there's nothing quite like a brisk space-walk!' grins the Doctor. 'Let's see where it's taken us...'

He releases the inner doors, and you step out into area cluttered with a variety of tools and equipment — drums of cabling, cans of lubricant, a grimy-looking lathe with a laser cutting tool. The carcass of a small vehicle, stripped down for repair, is supported by a levitating platform against one wall. Further along the same wall is a glowing Zoob entrance.

Unfortunately, you're not alone. At a nearby bench, two silver-eyed humanoids are busy rewiring a service drone. At your appearance, they abandon their work and stride menacingly towards you.

To grab a wrench from a tool rack, and prepare to defend yourself, go to 55. To dash for the Zoob, go to 87.

28 As you pretend to continue to be unconscious, one of your silver-eyed guards speaks to his companion.

'These unskinned humans must not be allowed to compromise the Colonising Initiative. We have the young one. When the other surrenders, we will graft them both.'

'Afraid I'm not the surrendering type!'

The Doctor is perched on top of the Fat Lady behind you, legs extended in front of him, his antidote device trained on your Shiner captors. He shuffles forward, and comes sliding fast down the ship's smooth hull, letting loose two antidote charges as he descends. By the time he lands lightly beside you, both Shiners have slumped to the hangar floor.

Pulling out his sonic screwdriver, the Doctor quickly releases your bonds. Several more Shiners are already hurrying across the hangar towards you.

To stand and fight, go to 24. To duck under the Fat Lady's low belly and hurriedly retreat, go to 12.

A shock awaits you beyond the phone box's doors. It seems the stranger's peculiar 'TARDIS' device really has transported you somewhere. It now stands within a futuristic-looking triangular room. Doorways in two of its walls lead to narrow corridors. In the third wall there is a strange round opening filled with dazzling green light.

A black plinth stands at the centre of the room. Floating impossibly above it is a complex geometric configuration, made up of twelve white spheres, connected in pairs by dark grey rods. The linked spheres are arranged in a twisting formation, rather like a section of DNA helix.

The Doctor moves forward and tentatively reaches out towards the floating helix. As he touches one of the rods connecting the spheres, it flares with red light, and a synthetic voice speaks.

'ZOOB 4J. FOR TRANSIT BETWEEN GEMINI APEX AND SCORPIO APEX. STATUS: ACTIVE. ENERGY RESERVES: FULL. ACCESS SETTING: SKINTHETIC PERSONNEL.'

You ask the Doctor what he thinks the device is.

'I'm not sure. I do know that a "Zoob" is a way of getting from one place to another — a Zoom Tube. That's one over there.' He points to the glowing opening. 'Moves you along a fixed path between two points at high speed.'

He looks thoughtful.

'Zoobs were mostly used in twenty-third century space stations. If these connectors represent Zoobs, I guess the twelve spheres must be operational units of some sort – these so-called "Apexes". Which would make this is a scale model of where we are – a space station layout map.'

He moves across to the glowing opening in the wall.

'I haven't used one of these for a long time. If I remember rightly, it's best to close your eyes. Helps reduce the acceleration sickness.'

To try the Zoob, go to 8. To explore the helix layout map further, go to 67.

30 As you head off alone, it's not long before you're wondering whether splitting up was such a good idea. The area your exploration leads you into is eerily silent. You can feel your heart beating fast against your ribs.

Suddenly, a figure steps out from nowhere to bar your path. It fixes you with a cold silver stare. You spin, only to find a second Shiner right behind you.

As this second assailant lunges at you, you dodge, and catch him while he's off-balance, sending him sprawling. But the other Shiner moves swiftly, wrapping his shimmering arm around your neck, and pinning your own behind your back.

The attacker you've just floored gets to his feet and confronts you, his inhuman eyes expressionless.

'We will prepare this human for grafting. Then we will seek the others.'

To continue to resist, go to 78. To submit, to avoid being treated roughly, go to 52.

31 In a sudden roar of rocket thrusters, the entire front section of the small spacecraft separates from its main body and shoots forward across the hangar with terrifying acceleration.

You are vaguely aware of Shiners and service drones scattering before you, and of hurtling narrowly past the Fat Lady's side, before the opposite hangar wall comes racing to meet you. An instant later, everything goes black.

You come round to find that you are no longer strapped in your seat. Instead, you are lying a little distance from where the smouldering wreck of the craft's escape pod lies crumpled against the hangar wall.

Blip is crouching over you.

'I managed to drag you clear. Couldn't get back for the Doctor before there were Shiners all over it, though.'

He begins to help you up.

'Come on — we need to find somewhere to lie low...'

**To find cover, as Blip suggests, go to 50.
To try to help the Doctor, go to 88.**

You dive through the box's narrow doors. What you find inside makes your head spin. You appear to have entered a huge, cavernous chamber.

As you gawp at your surroundings uncomprehendingly, there's a series of loud thwumps against the walls, followed by squeals of protest from the chamber's strange superstructure.

'She's wrapping herself around the TARDIS,' says the stranger, striding onto a central raised platform which holds a circular console. He hurriedly begins adjusting some of its many bizarre-looking controls.

'We need to get moving. She'll not be able to cling on for long once we're in transit.'

You finally find your voice.

'What was that thing?'

'Lesser Constrictorix. Nasty piece of work. Not as bad as the Greater variety, obviously, but still no pussycat. Fingers crossed we can shake her off in some uninhabited time zone...'

'And who are you?'

The man looks up from the control panel and beams at you.

'I'm the Doctor.'

He throws a final switch, and the chamber suddenly fills with an oscillating whooshing sound. For several seconds, you experience a peculiar juddering motion. Then everything falls still.

The Doctor cups a hand behind his ear theatrically. All is quiet.

'That should have done the trick. Only a relatively small space/time-hop, but I think we can safely say we no longer have an unwanted passenger.'

He gestures to the doors.

'Shall we see where we are?'

To lead the way out of the TARDIS doors, go to 17. To let the Doctor go first, go to 53.

You hurry after the Doctor, who quickly leads you to a place where three Zoob openings glow alongside one another. The Doctor halts in front of them.

'Now then, unless I'm much mistaken, the one we want is... that one!'

He strides confidently into the central Zoob, and vanishes. Remembering the Doctor's anti-sickness tip, you take a moment to prepare yourself, then follow.

The Doctor's intuition hasn't failed him — the Zoob does indeed take you to the area you originally arrived in, where the TARDIS still stands. Only now, the Doctor's magical blue box is surrounded by a host of silver-eyed Shiners.

Two of the creatures are already grappling with the Doctor. As he manages to wrestle free momentarily, he turns to you, wild-eyed.

'It's a trap! Get out of here!'

To attempt to help the Doctor, go to 4.
To quickly turn and re-enter the Zoob, go to 80.

34 The blue stuff is surprisingly nice. As you enjoy it, the Doctor offers his hand to your new friend.

'Thanks for getting us out of a tight spot. I'm the Doctor.'

The boy gives a humph.

'I'm Blip. Afraid I'm not mad keen on doctors.'

'Why's that, Blip?'

'I'm hypomelanomic, ain't I. Ain't got enough pigment in my cells. That's why my hair and skin are so pale. I've had doctors poking and prodding me ever since I was born. It was a doctor what sent me here. Reckoned one of these "Second Skin" grafts might help me out.'

'What's "Second Skin"?'

'The big idea of the company that owns this place. It's this artificial skin that's meant to protect you from the effects of sunlight — what with the ozone layer having completely vanished now, and everybody having to deal with the cancer risk all the time — 'specially people like me. They stick a patch of this UV-proof Second Skin on your chest, and it grows to cover your whole body.'

Blip gives a brief shiver.

'Only I saw what it done to the others that tested it. After a couple of days, their eyes silvered over, and they started acting weird. Shiners, I call 'em. So I did a runner. Since then the Shiners have been forcing everyone else on board to have a graft. Reckon we're the only normal folk left.'

The Doctor looks concerned.

'I think we'd better find out all we can about this Second Skin project — and fast.'

To split up, to see what evidence you can find, go to 30. To search together, go to 91.

35 As you wriggle forwards towards the junction in the narrow duct, there's an unsettling creaking noise, and the surface beneath you gives way. You and the Doctor fall helplessly though the air, landing in a tangled heap.

You pick yourselves up slowly, bruised, but not badly hurt. The robotic arm you observed in action has broken off its surgical task. A lens at its tip is pointing directly at you, in a robotic stare.

'Hi,' beams the Doctor, brushing debris from his suit. 'Hope you don't mind us dropping in!'

A small red light beside the eye-lens begins to flash, and an ear-splitting alarm bursts into life.

You rush from the strange operating theatre into the passageway outside. But two pairs of silver-eyed humanoids are already responding to the alarm, converging on you from opposite ends of the corridor.

To prepare to fight them off, go to 55.
To attempt to barge past one pair, go to 7.

'That's a good question,' says the Doctor. 'However, a more pressing one, I think you'll agree, is who on Gallifrey is he?'

Following his concerned gaze, you see a lone figure rapidly approaching. At a distance, he seems unremarkable, an ordinary man. But as he strides nearer, you notice that he has one chillingly inhuman feature — his eyes are silver, and have no iris or pupil.

As he comes to a halt before you, the Doctor greets him with a broad grin, offering his hand.

'Glad to make your acquaintance. I'm the Doctor.'

The silver-eyed humanoid pauses momentarily, then responds by also extending a hand — but only to grasp the Doctor by the throat. At close range, you can see that the skin on the creature's arm has an inhuman sheen to it, shimmering eerily.

As the Doctor claws at the stranger's hand, wide-eyed and desperate to breathe, you try to help — only to be sent sprawling across the floor by a blow from the creature's other powerful arm. You collide painfully with a stack of metallic canisters, and quickly hurry to regain your feet, determined to help the Doctor.

To use one of the heavy canisters to attack the Doctor's assailant, go to 59. To try to make it clear that you both submit, go to 22.

37 As you reach the small spacecraft, the Doctor hits its hatch release. You slip inside, and clamber into the cramped cockpit's twin seats. The Doctor begins hastily tapping at the control screens suspended in front of him.

'Let's see if we can get this tin can moving.'

Then mayhem breaks loose. A piercing alarm screams into life, and a thick silver restraint curls around your abdomen, pinning you to your seat. An alert flashes angrily on the central display screen:

BIOMETRIC IDENTIFICATION FAILED

SYSTEM LOCKDOWN INITIATED

'I can't get anything to respond!'

The Doctor rips the face from a control panel, and begins poking around inside with his sonic screwdriver.

Through the cockpit window, you can see Shiners and drones rapidly converging on your small ship.

'Got it!' yells the Doctor, as two red buttons beside each pilot's seat suddenly illuminate. 'I can't override the lockdown, but I've got the emergency escape systems back online.' He gives you a forced smile. 'It won't be pretty, but they might just get us out of here.'

> **To hit the button marked EMERGENCY EJECT, go to 61. To choose the ESCAPE POD button, go to 31.**

38 You hurry away along a deserted corridor, until it meets another at a T-junction. There is an alcove in the wall at this intersection, housing a bank of eight narrow bays. In each stands a machine that looks a bit like a moped without wheels.

'Air scooters,' says the Doctor. 'They're power-charging, by the looks of it.'

A small coloured light glows in each scooter's side. The Doctor moves to the end of the row, where two vehicles have green lights. As he grasps the first scooter's handgrips, it rises to hover thirty centimetres above the floor.

'These'll help us get around a bit faster,' smiles the Doctor. He guides the hovering vehicle from its bay and climbs on. 'Go on — have a try!'

You withdraw and mount the second charged scooter. As you settle into its saddle, it bobs gently in mid-air.

To fly the scooter along the left-hand corridor, go to 51. To try the other direction, go to 56.

39 | Clutching his psychic paper, the Doctor steps out into the corridor.

'Sorry to alarm you, sir. As you can see from my papers, I'm Officer Jacobs of the Lunar Prison Authority. We have reason to believe that two dangerous convicts have found their way aboard this facility. We're gathering all personnel in Virgo Apex for a detailed briefing. I'd appreciate it if you could make your way there immediately.'

The Doctor's delivery is superb — you almost believe him. But the response is a flat, monotone statement.

'You have not been grafted.'

'I apologise for any inconvenience, but it's essential that we assemble as quickly as —'

'All humans must be grafted.'

'Ah.'

You sense from the Doctor's tone that the game is up. Bursting from hiding, you charge at the surprised humanoid, and manage to knock him down, sending the weapon he had trained on the Doctor spilling from his grasp.

'Plan B!' yells the Doctor. 'RUN!'

> **To sprint along the corridor the way you came, go to 83. To flee in the other direction, go to 58.**

40 The floor lurches suddenly, throwing you off balance. A peculiar oscillating whoosh begins to rise and fall over an underlying mechanical thrum.

'Now we're cooking!' the stranger yells cheerily at you over the din, somehow keeping his feet as the floor shudders again. 'I'm the Doctor, by the way. Welcome aboard!'

After a few seconds, the sounds and motion suddenly cease. The 'Doctor' bends to consult one of the bizarre instruments on his control console.

'Ah.' He sounds a little hesitant. 'Slight miscalculation on my part. I was aiming for a minor spatial translation — sort of side step out of the danger area. But we appear to have moved a little further than I intended. And not just spatially...'

He gives you a sheepish grin.

'According to these readouts, we're now orbiting Earth at an altitude of around 350 kilometres, in the year 2225. Ooops.'

Clearly this 'Doctor' character is a little unhinged. You're suddenly keen to discover whether the creature outside has gone, so you can return to the safety and sanity of home.

To humour the stranger with an 'if you say so' look, go to 81. To hurry for the doorway, go to 29.

41 | 'Cracked it!'

As Blip finally succeeds in hot-wiring the pod's electronic lock, its lid hisses open. Inside are hundreds of silver canisters. Blip pulls one out, opens it, and withdraws a slim transparent casing containing a thin patch of skin-like tissue.

'Nice work, young man!'

The Doctor is standing in the doorway.

'Wish I'd made as much progress. Haven't found my way back to the TARDIS yet — this place is a labyrinth! Think I've got my bearings now, though. You two wait here with the patch. I'll be back with my diagnostic stuff in a jiffy.'

Moments after the Doctor hurries away, a Zoob flares into life in the far wall of the laboratory. You and Blip dive for cover as three Shiners emerge from it. As they move out into the lab, Blip gestures silently to the Zoob, and begins crawling towards it.

To crawl after Blip to the Zoob, go to 11.
To sneak to the door and go after the Doctor, go to 33.

Holding your nose (and feeling ridiculous) you step into the Zoob. You experience a momentary lurching sensation — like a roller-coaster ride compressed into a split second — before staggering forward into an entirely new area.

The room in which you've emerged is dominated by a large transparent dome. Sealed inside it is a hexagonal plinth, on which you can see a shallow plastic dish — the sort used for growing biological cultures. You can just make out a small patch of almost-colourless tissue resting on the jelly-like substance within the dish.

Suspended above the tiny tissue patch is a strange mechanical device. Each of its numerous robotic arms carries a miniature camera, scalpel, syringe, or other scientific tool.

There is a console beside the dome incorporating several control screens and a binocular-like viewfinder. You guess this is the interface by which the device inside is operated.

To ask the Doctor what he thinks the device is for, go to 36. To take a look through its viewfinder, go to 16.

43 The Doctor hasn't gone far when a volley of laser blasts suddenly strike the side of his robo-loader. A group of Shiners have emerged from behind the Fat Lady, and have him in their laser-rifle sights.

The Doctor urges his damaged machine onwards, but as a second wave of laser fire cuts across its mechanical legs, it crashes to the floor. The Shiners begin making their way towards the wrecked loader.

Your heart skips a beat as you are suddenly aware of someone's presence beside you.

'That's torn it! Now he's in real trouble.'

It's Blip. As he crouches beside you, you quickly suggest that by distracting the Shiner's attention, you might give the Doctor a chance to escape. Blip looks doubtful.

'Chances are we'll all end up caught. Maybe we should bide our time. Lay low till there's a better chance to help him…'

To try to divert the Shiners' attention, go to 88. To lie low, as Blip suggests, go to 50.

44 You continue to observe the strange humanoids from your hiding place. It isn't long before all the cylindrical canisters have been gathered and packed. Both fully-laden white pods gently rise to hover a metre or so above the floor.

The humanoids guide the floating pods towards the exit, and out into the corridor beyond. As the last figure leaves the lab, the doors slice firmly shut.

The Doctor hurries to the doorway, withdrawing his sonic screwdriver. As he touches it to a control panel in the wall, there's a shower of blue sparks.

'Rats! It's crypto-locked. This might take a while. But we can't risk going back through the Zoob...'

You scan the area for an alternative exit. There are no other doors. But there is a grilled opening in the centre of the laboratory's ceiling — a ventilation duct.

To give the Doctor longer to crack the door lock, go to 26. To suggest that you escape via the ventilation duct, go to 72.

You sprint towards the Fat Lady, following the anti-grav conveyor that is feeding the last cargo pods into her cavernous hold. Up ahead, between you and the hold's entrance, you can see another group of Shiners. Their attention is currently on the ship's interior, but it seems impossible that you can pass without confronting them.

'Quick — up here!'

The Doctor leaps up into the narrow gap between two of the moving pods. You follow his lead, and find yourself riding the invisible force field that supports the pods. It's weird — like surfing or skateboarding without a board.

As the Doctor resets the antidote device, you consider your next move. Even hidden between the cargo pods, you're sure to be spotted by the Shiners guarding the hold.

To jump down at the last minute and engage them, go to 12. To scramble up on top of the pod in front of you, to be better hidden, go to 25.

As you and the Doctor go to leave the room, a loud sneeze makes you both jump. The Doctor spins, raising his sonic screwdriver.

'Who's there?'

A boy, not more than nine years old, slowly emerges from his hiding place. He has very pale skin, and a striking mop of white hair.

The Doctor lowers his sonic.

'And who might you be, my young friend?'

'I'm Blip.' The boy stares into the Doctor's eyes, then yours. His own eyes have an unusual purplish tinge. 'You're not Shiners, are you?'

'Not what?'

'Shiners. It's what I call them things that the patches turn you into. It's the same with everyone that's tested 'em. Their skin goes all shimmery, their eyes silver over, and they start acting weird. I was supposed to be a tester, too, 'cos of me being hypomelanomic. I ain't got enough pigment in my skin cells, so the sun's even more dangerous for me. They reckoned a Second Skin graft might help. But I didn't fancy it — did a runner. Since then the Shiners have taken over. Everyone on board's been forced to have a graft — 'cept you and me.'

The Doctor looks concerned.

'I think, Blip, that we'd better find out all we can about this Second Skin project — and fast.'

To split up, to see what evidence you can find, go to 30. To search together, go to 91.

Entering the right-hand Zoob sends you on another split-second, stomach-churning journey. You emerge onto a narrow platform overlooking a vast open chamber. In its far side, a pair of massive sliding doors are slowly revealing the star-pricked blackness of space beyond. This is the Leo Apex hangar area. At the centre of the hangar floor is a colossal barrel-shaped spacecraft.

'The Fat Lady,' the Doctor reads on the ship's hull. 'Surface-to-orbit freighter, by the looks of her. There go our patches, look…'

He points to a hatch high in the ship's near side. A stream of large white cargo pods are being conveyed by a monorail-like track that runs from below the platform on which you are standing. The moving pods float just below the track, with no visible attachment to it. On reaching the entrance to the Fat Lady's hold, they drop slowly into the ship's interior.

Overseeing the loading procedure are several dozen Shiners, assisted by as many service drones.

'We could try to get to the launch doors and jam them,' suggests the Doctor. 'Or perhaps sabotage the cargo loading system. One way or another, we've got to stop her launching. Those pods hold enough Second Skin patches to mutate half the planet.'

To attempt to sabotage the loading system, go to 76. To make your way down to the hangar floor, and sneak across to the main doors, go to 25.

You crawl along the duct's left-hand junction until you reach another grille. The Doctor peers through it.

'Looks like there's nobody around.'

He quickly removes the grille and drops silently into the room below. You follow suit, landing lightly beside him.

You're standing in the central aisle of a long, narrow room, walled in on both sides by tall white cabinets. There are doorways at either end of the aisle, and a glowing Zoob entrance midway along it.

Each cabinet has a numerical keypad. You experimentally tap a few digits into the nearest one. A small foil-wrapped cube is instantly dispensed into a hopper at the base of the cabinet. The Doctor retrieves it, and reads its label.

'Meal 85. Macaroni Cheese. Rehydration guidelines: 10 seconds, setting 2.' He grins at you. 'I guess we're in the pantry.'

His smile dissolves as two silver-eyed figures appear in the doorway at the far end of the aisle.

To dash for the Zoob entrance, go to 87.
To attempt to topple over one of the food dispensers, to create a delay, go to 91.

As you step into the glowing opening, an invisible fist closes around your insides, yanking you forward with a sickening jolt. An instant later, you stagger forward into entirely different surroundings.

The Doctor, beside you, grins at your bewildered expression.

'What did you make of your first trip by Zoob then, eh?'

You look blank.

'Zoobs. Zoom Tubes. They're the twenty-third century forerunner of the teleport. Transport you along a fixed path between two points at ultra-high velocity. Best to hold your breath when you use one — reduces the nausea.'

The Zoob has brought you to a passageway that leads to an opening a little distance ahead. As you and the Doctor approach the opening, a small black sphere drops from above to block your path into the chamber beyond. An illuminated palm shape appears on its upper surface as an artificial voice addresses you:

'WELCOME TO SAGITTARIUS APEX. THIS IS A RECORDED ACCESS AREA. PLEASE USE THE PALM-PAD INTERFACE TO LOG IN.'

To ignore the device, and move on into the chamber to search for clues as to where the TARDIS has brought you, go to 94. To obey the device, go to 16.

As you and Blip watch anxiously from your hiding place, a siren sounds, and the Fat Lady's cargo doors begin to close. The Shiners and service drones around her move off, quickly vacating the hangar via its exit doors, which seal behind them.

Moments later, there's a crackling roar as the spacecraft's rockets ignite. She rises, and rides on a cushion of fire towards the open hangar doors. As she moves smoothly out into open space beyond, Blip gives a defeated sigh.

'That's it then. Millions of patches. Earth'll be overrun…'

'Don't throw in the towel just yet, my friend!'

Somehow, the Doctor has appeared beside you. He is clutching a reel of thin cable. He looks rather dishevelled, but determination is blazing in his eyes.

'The Fat Lady is a beam-rider,' explains the Doctor as he strides quickly to the hangar doors. 'She follows a flight path projected by a transmitter. That transmitter.' He points out to where a gantry protrudes from the space station's hull. There is a large aerial-like device at its tip.

'If I can tweak the transmitter, I can change the flight-path. She's meant to touch down at Earthport Nine, in Florida. But I've got other plans.'

He hurriedly ties one end of the cable around his waist,

passes you the other, and moves to the threshold of the hangar. Close up, you can see that a transparent film forms a barrier between the pressurised atmosphere of the hangar and the vacuum of space beyond.

'Once I'm past the pressure field, I'll have no oxygen. Give me one minute, then haul me in.'

With that, the Doctor launches himself into open space. You watch anxiously as he drifts the thirty metres or so to the gantry, grasps it, and clambers awkwardly to the transmitter at its tip. Blip counts out the seconds.

'Now!'

At Blip's cue, you pull the cable in quickly, dragging the Doctor back across the void. As he clears the pressure field, he collapses, breathless, on the hangar floor.

'Did it!… Just a slight realignment… Should be enough… Unless I'm much mistaken, she's now destined for a rather damp landing. Smack bang in the middle of the Gulf of Mexico. And immersion in salt water is one thing our exo-parasitic friends won't survive.'

He gets to his feet and gives Blip a broad grin.

'You see — never say die! It's not over till the Fat Lady sinks!'

His expression becomes serious.

'Right then — next job is to get you two kitted out with antidote guns, so you can help me clear up the Shiners left on board. Then I'd better get you both home in the TARDIS. We could maybe take a slight detour, but not for too long...'

He grins at you both.

'Otherwise your folks will skin me!'

THE END

The air scooters carry you swiftly along the corridor, until it opens into a huge chamber. At its centre stands a cluster of massive black columns, the uppermost ends of which emit a fiery orange glow. The Doctor leads you in a looping climb, circling the device.

'Some kind of reactor,' he yells, pulling alongside you. 'Must be the station's main power plant.'

Suddenly, a bolt of red light fizzes out of nowhere to strike the rear end of the Doctor's scooter. Lurching to one side, it collides with yours, sending you careering out of control.

Unable to recover from your spiralling dive, you hit the chamber floor hard, and are flung from your scooter's saddle. The Doctor, too, is sent sprawling. As you pick yourselves up, dazed, you see a group of laser-toting humanoids hurriedly making their way towards you.

To attempt to get your scooter airborne again, go to 7. To square up to the advancing humanoids, go to 55.

52 | You cooperate with the Shiners as they escort you along a corridor, then bundle you into a small room containing only a bench-like bed. As one of the Shiners shoves you forward, another punches a keypad on the wall. Vertical bars of blue light suddenly enclose the portion of room you're in.

The first Shiner speaks to you through the crackling bars.

'You will be detained here until we have prepared a grafting theatre.'

Then they leave.

Minutes later, the cell door opens again. This time, to your great relief, it's Blip. He hurries to the keypad, and the blue energy bars flicker out of life.

'Come on — I've got a patch!'

He leads you out into the corridor.

'We need to track down the Doctor — which way do you reckon?'

He hesitates, then without waiting for an answer, heads left.

To follow Blip, go to 19. To try the other direction, go to 64.

'Get down!'

The Doctor's warning comes as you follow him out of the TARDIS doors. You instinctively hit the deck — just as a bolt of red light fizzes over your head and explodes against the TARDIS behind you.

To your bewilderment, your surroundings have completely changed. You now appear to be midway along a corridor. Its mirrored walls are featureless but for a strange circular opening, veiled by a curtain of purple light.

A few metres away stands what looks like a pedal-bin with six spider-like mechanical legs. As you watch from your prone position, it lets loose another red energy bolt, which narrowly misses you.

Clasping his sonic screwdriver, the Doctor scrambles forward and lunges at the killer-bin. As the sonic's tip makes contact with it, all six of its limbs instantly go limp, and it slumps to the floor.

The Doctor blows out his cheeks in relief.

'Security drone. Obviously not impressed by our unannounced arrival.'

He prises open a panel in the robot's back, and begins to scan its electronic innards.

'Let's see if we can brighten its mood a bit. Security Mode... Cleansing Mode... Ah! Here we go — Hospitality Mode...'

As the robotic device reactivates, it rises once more onto its multiple legs. To your amusement, it begins to speak in the soft, silky voice of a human female.

'On behalf of Skinthetic Corporation, welcome aboard our Iso-Sphere headquarters. This unique Earth-orbiting facility boasts the very latest in twenty-third century technology. Its 12 operational units are arranged at the apexes of an isohedral configuration. All Apex units are linked by a state-of-the-art rapid-transit system. Visitors are advised that use of this Zoom Tube network is at their own risk. Have a nice day.'

And with that, the drone turns and scuttles away.

To explore your surroundings further, go to 93. To try the glowing opening, go to 57.

As you head for the hangar doors, a bolt of red laser fire suddenly cuts across your path. Before you can take cover, a second blast hits the floor just in front of your feet. The explosion throws up a shower of debris, and sends you sprawling. You hit your head hard, and everything goes black.

When you gradually come to, head swimming sickeningly, it is to find yourself slouched in the shadow of the Fat Lady's vast belly. Your hands and feet are shackled with hi-tech restraints.

Two figures stand nearby, their backs to you. Though you cannot see their eyes, the skin on the back of their necks has a telltale sheen. You appear to be a captive of the Shiners.

There's no sign of the Doctor.

To attempt to get to your feet, go to 82.
To remain motionless, pretending to still be unconscious, go to 28.

55 You square up to the advancing humanoids, pulse racing. Out of nowhere, a scruffy-looking boy, not more than nine years old, appears. He is clutching a device made of a bundle of electronic components lashed to a transparent flask. Lobbing the device, the boy yells at you and the Doctor.

'Follow me!'

As you obey, there is a loud explosion followed by wailing and grunting. You don't look back, but keep pace as he leads you along a corridor before halting abruptly. With a whack of his fist, he releases a panel in the wall, shepherds you and the Doctor through, then follows, replacing the panel behind him. You find yourself in a cramped but concealed den.

'Nice place,' says the Doctor. 'And splendid work back there, young man.'

'Slime grenade,' says the boy with a grin. 'Knocked it up myself. It won't hurt 'em — they're human, underneath, you see.'

He grabs a half-unwrapped block of chunky blue stuff lying nearby and thrusts it at you cheerfully.

'Hungry?'

To accept his offer of food, go to 34.
To politely decline, go to 71.

You get the hang of the air scooter quite quickly — the left handgrip controls your speed, the right one alters you altitude. As you and the Doctor fly side by side along the corridor, your anxiety eases — this is fun!

Suddenly a luminous bolt of energy fizzes narrowly past you. Looking over your shoulder, you see a group of three scooter-mounted figures in hot pursuit.

'Down here!' yells the Doctor, sending his scooter into a swooping turn into a side corridor. As you follow, your heart sinks. It's a dead end. Ahead, the corridor terminates in a glowing opening — a Zoob.

Reaching the end of the corridor, you bring your scooters to a halt, and hurriedly dismount — just as your pursuers hurtle around the corner behind you, firing as they come.

To jam your scooter's speed control and launch it at your pursuers, to delay them, go to 21. To make straight for the Zoob, go to 87.

57 You step into the light-filled opening, and immediately experience the sensation of being seized by your innards and wrenched forward with tremendous force. A moment later, you stumble forward into an entirely unfamiliar area.

As you concentrate on keeping your breakfast down, the Doctor emerges behind you, removing his fingers from his ears.

'Wa-hey! Now that's the way to travel!'

He turns to look at the glowing opening admiringly.

'Of course, once they crack teleportation, nobody will be interested in these anymore. Zoom Tubes, they're called. "Zoobs", for short. Transport you along a fixed path at ultra-high speed. They must use them to get from one Apex to another quickly.'

He notices that you're a little green.

'Top tip — blocking your ears stops the transit sickness. Haven't the faintest idea why, but there you are...'

To take a moment to recover from your Zoob ride, go to 89. To push on with exploring the area it has taken you to, go to 20.

You dash along the corridor, then down another, managing to put a little distance between yourselves and your pursuer — but unable to shake him off completely.

Then, turning a corner, you almost charge headlong into a vehicle — a high-tech baggage van — hovering unattended at one side of the corridor. Its train of levitating trailers are stacked high with white canisters, all carrying a SKINTHETIC logo.

'Look!'

The Doctor points to the corridor ceiling. Directly above the loaded vehicle is a grilled opening, large enough for a person to squeeze through.

'I'll soon fetch that grille off,' says the Doctor. 'If we hide up there, we might lose old Silver Eyes!'

You're not sure there's time — the sound of footfalls from around the corner is drawing rapidly closer.

To clamber up a canister stack to reach the ceiling grille, go to 72. To overturn one of the trailers, so the spilt canisters block the corridor, go to 21.

Your blow sends the strange humanoid staggering backwards, causing it to release its grip around the Doctor's neck. The Doctor reels drunkenly for a few moments, gulping down air, then turns to you urgently.

'Move!'

You don't need telling twice. The Doctor's assailant has also recovered, and has now drawn a hi-tech firearm.

You spin and dodge away — just in time to avoid a fizzing bolt of energy. As the creature takes aim again, the Doctor whips out his sonic screwdriver and raises it to eye level. This time, the energy bolt is on target. But as it hurtles towards you, it is deflected, ricocheting back to strike the humanoid, who slumps to the floor.

The Doctor hurries forward to examine the unconscious creature.

'My deflector shield took some of the sting out of it — he's just stunned.'

'Doctor!'

You've spotted a second approaching figure. He has the same shimmering skin and silver eyes as your original attacker.

The Doctor quickly delves in another suit pocket and pulls out what appears to be a blank piece of paper.

'There's a chance this might work. Psychic paper. If we're lucky, it'll make old Shiny Eyes believe whatever I tell him. We could bluff our way out. Or we take our only other option — leg it!'

To run for it, go to 83. To bluff your way out of your predicament, go to 13.

60 After a short distance, the corridor leads to a pair of sliding doors. As you approach them, they glide apart automatically — and you come to a dead halt. Immediately beyond the doors, a lone figure stands in the corridor.

Only when several seconds pass, and the figure remains motionless, does your panic subside. For some reason, the man seems completely unaware of you and the Doctor. As you approach cautiously, you can see that his eyes are shut.

'Look at his skin.'

You understand why the Doctor is intrigued. Wherever the man's skin is exposed, it has an unnatural sheen to it, almost as though it is shimmering.

The Doctor carefully scans his sonic screwdriver across the man's body. It's blue light pulses very slowly.

'His metabolic readings are way too low — it's like he's in hibernation. And I'm picking up non-human bio-signs...'

Even as he speaks, the sonic's pulses begin to accelerate. Moments later, the man's eyes flick open. And you suddenly realise that this isn't a man. No human has such nightmarish eyes — metallic silver, without iris or pupil.

Before either of you can react, the creature reaches out with a shimmering-skinned arm and grasps the Doctor by the throat.

**To try to reason with the strange humanoid,
to prevent it harming the Doctor, go to 22.
To shoulder charge it, go to 59.**

61 You press the 'emergency eject' button, and your seat unit rockets through a hatch in the cabin's roof. The seat sails through the air, clean over the hulking body of the Fat Lady below. As you begin to descend, the hangar floor rushes up to meet you. But at the last minute, your landing is cushioned by automatic mini-thrusters incorporated in the device.

As you struggle to free yourself from the ejector seat's restraint, a small, white-haired figure ducks out from behind a vehicle hovering unattended nearby, and hurries to help you.

'Nice flying!' grins Blip, prising open the restraint. 'Was that the Doctor in the other one? Didn't look like he was so lucky — landed right in the middle of a bunch of Shiners. They'll be all over here in a minute, too — better find somewhere to lie low pretty sharpish.'

To do as Blip suggests, go to 50. To go to the Doctor's aid, go to 88.

From your hiding place, you watch the approach of several figures. As they draw nearer, you suppress an involuntary gasp of shock. Though their basic anatomy is humanoid, they have one distinctly inhuman feature — their eyes are metallic silver, with no iris or pupil.

There is something else strange about the silver-eyed figures. Wherever their skin is exposed, it appears to shimmer slightly.

The group halts only a few metres away. The lead figure scans the corridor ahead with his blank silver-eyed stare, then addresses his companions.

'We will deactivate all Zoom Tubes from this sector. The intruders must be apprehended and taken to the Grafting Theatre.'

The other figures separate wordlessly into two groups, and move off in opposite directions along the corridor. As they depart, the remaining figure — the speaker — wrenches a panel from the corridor wall beside him and thrusts a hand inside. A moment later, the glow of the Zoob entrance beside you fades and dies.

As you exchange anxious looks with the Doctor, he delves in his suit pocket and pulls out a blank piece of paper.

'Psychic paper. We could try to bluff our way past him,'

he hisses, in a barely audible whisper. Then he gestures to a grille in the low ceiling above you.

'Otherwise, I guess the only way is up...'

To go along with whatever bluff the Doctor has up his sleeve, go to 39. To climb up into the service void above the corridor, go to 72.

63 The Doctor checks his antidote device is charged, tosses it to you, and withdraws his sonic screwdriver.

'Okay my young friend — let's bag ourselves a couple of cosmobots!'

Together you break from cover and charge at the group of Shiners. You fire off your first antidote charge, and one of them hits the deck.

The Shiners are quick to respond. As their laser blasts flash towards you, the Doctor raises his sonic screwdriver, and the bolts of red energy are deflected harmlessly away.

Unfortunately, the cosmobots appear to be armed, too. Laser fire is soon coming at you and the Doctor so thick and fast that you are driven back.

'Time for a Plan B!' yells the Doctor. 'Either we make a dash for the ship's hold, or...'

He gestures to a smaller spacecraft docked at the far side of the hangar.

'... or we could try to use that maintenance tug to block the launch doors, so the Fat Lady can't take off. What d'you think?'

To dash for the Fat Lady's hold, go to 45. To head for the maintenance craft, go to 37.

As Blip rushes off in one direction, you take the other, keen to find the Doctor as quickly as possible.

You're in luck. In only the second room you search, a familiar figure stands hunched over a bank of computer screens.

'Doctor!'

He raises a hand in greeting, without averting his gaze from the data scrolling across the screen in front of him.

'This is fascinating stuff. An encrypted archive. There's a full log of research activities — notes kept by the top bod here, a Professor Tivez. Turns out Skinthetic didn't manufacture a synthetic skin at all. Tivez found it. In a fragment of comet ice. A small patch of tissue. Ran tests on it, and discovered it exhibited UV resistance and a whole load of other interesting properties. He saw the commercial possibilities, and set up Skinthetic. The Second Skin patches are all cloned from the cluster of cells he originally dug up.'

The Doctor looks up at you.

'Tivez must have known that the tissue was alien. What he doesn't appear to have realised is that it wasn't skin. I recognise the molecular structure from his SEM scans. What he found was a small hibernating colony of exo-parasites — organisms that live by encapsulating a living host of another species and hijacking their biological resources.

By cloning Second Skin patches, he's replicated the exo-parasites a billion-fold.'

He stoops over the data screen once more.

'And according to this, the first bulk shipment of patches is being loaded aboard an orbital freighter in Capricorn Apex right now. Fifty million of them, intended for a global market.'

He grabs a strange firearm-like device from where it lies on the console beside him, and points purposefully at a Zoob in the far wall of the room.

'Which is why we need to get to the hangar area pronto. If we don't stop that ship leaving, your entire race is going to be overrun.'

To ask what the device is, go to 77. To ask what the plan is once you reach the hangar, go to 23.

Blip is still searching the system files for clues as to the whereabouts and origins of the Second Skin patches, when a Zoob suddenly flares into life in the opposite wall. As two Shiners step from it, you dive for cover. Crouching behind a computer terminal, you listen to the creatures' conversation.

'We must initiate the first colonising wave. The patches have been cloned and packaged, and await dispatch.'

'Let us issue the command to our brothers and sisters to begin the loading procedure.'

As the Shiners cross to a multiple touchscreen console, you and Blip creep silently away. You manage to sneak to the room's doorway, without being noticed. In the corridor outside, Blip whispers urgently to you.

'We've got to find the Doctor — warn him not to come back here! I'll try this way...'

And he hurries off.

To follow him, go to 19. To follow the corridor in the other direction, go to 30.

You reach the hangar floor, and quietly slip behind a stack of metal containers. As you do so, you notice the rumbling of the opening hangar doors cease. They've reached their fully open position.

The rumbling sound is replaced by a gentler mechanical hum. The central section of the hangar floor begins to turn very slowly, gradually rotating the Fat Lady to face the open doors.

'Look!' whispers the Doctor. 'Over there, by the doors.'

He is pointing to a control console from which a Shiner is just moving away.

'They must be the turntable controls. If we can put them out of action before she's lined up, she'll not be able to launch.'

But you have a more immediate problem. A group of patrolling Shiners are heading in your direction.

To take on the Shiner patrol, go to 12.
To make a dash for the turntable control console, beside the hangar doors, go to 54.

You reach out to touch the illuminated Zoob on the model again, to see what happens. In response, it changes from red to green in colour. A hairline crack suddenly appears around a rectangular section of the previously featureless plinth beneath the model. The rectangular black slab slides silently forward, then slowly begins to rise, until it has formed a waist-high column.

As you and the Doctor exchange bemused looks, the synthetic voice speaks once more.

'TO EDIT SETTINGS FOR ZOOB 4J, PLEASE ENGAGE WITH CONTROL INTERFACE.'

Two areas of the column's smooth upper surface begin to glow warm red, rather like a ceramic hob. But instead of being circular, the glowing areas are palm-shaped.

To place your hands onto the control column, as instructed, go to 16. To ask the Doctor whether he thinks it's safe to do so, go to 36.

'Follow me,' says the Doctor. 'And keep low.'

Using whatever cover the stacks of equipment and supplies around the hangar provide, you make your way stealthily towards the Fat Lady. You duck behind a container and watch as another party of Shiners enters the hangar through an entrance in the far wall. The silver-eyed humanoids are escorting a floating platform, which carries a dozen slim, matt-black cylinders.

'Fuel cells,' the Doctor whispers. 'Once they've loaded those, she'll be all set to go.'

Your best chance of getting aboard the Fat Lady is an open access hatch in her starboard bow. But another Shiner is patrolling the area around this entrance. As you ponder your next move, this guard turns and begins striding purposefully towards your current hiding place.

To pick off the guard with a shot from the antidote device, go to 10. To stay hidden, go to 2.

Your hiding place proves inadequate. As the Shiners approach, Blip makes a desperate appeal.

'You're human, ain't yer? What have you got against us?'

The lead Shiner's mouth curls into a cruel smirk.

'Human? I think not. The bodies of your fellow humans survive within us, yes. But they are ours to control. Muscles, nerves, even this voice with which I speak — all are now governed by our superior intellect. And soon we will colonise all humans. A vessel is being made ready in this facility's hangar for departure to Earth. Its cargo comprises many millions of Second Skin patches, each one a proto-colony of my brothers and sisters. The patches will be distributed to eager consumers across your planet. Soon Earth's entire population will become hosts for my species.'

'Not if I can help it!'

The Doctor has appeared behind the Shiners, holding a peculiar device. Before they can react, he uses it to unleash a series of orange pulses. The Shiners slump to the floor and lie still.

The Doctor kneels beside the nearest unconscious figure.

'Won't have hurt them. It's an antidote charge, to inhibit the alien tissue. When they come round, they should be back to normal.'

'What alien tissue?' asks Blip.

'Their new skin. It's an exo-parasite — a sophisticated lifeform that colonises living hosts, hijacking their biological systems. Someone must have found the original tissue they cloned the Second Skin patches from on a non-terrestrial source. Piece of comet ice, probably. They've been messing with stuff they don't understand.'

He stands, and turns to Blip.

'We need to stop that cargo vessel being launched. Otherwise humankind is in serious trouble. Can you get us to the hangar area?'

Blip turns and scurries away. You and the Doctor hurry after him until you come to a place where twin Zoob openings glow brightly in the wall ahead.

'Those go to the two hangar Apexes — Leo and Pisces. Dunno which you need.'

The Doctor ruffles Blip's white hair. 'Nice job. One more thing. I knocked up this antidote device in a hurry. It's only got enough lithium cells for a few more charges. Do you think you could get your hands on any more?'

Blip nods resolutely, and hurries away.

To take the left-hand Zoob, go to 6. To take the right-hand one, go to 47.

Your first journey by Zoob feels bizarre — like being sucked very, very quickly through a tiny hole — but thanks to the Doctor's tip-off, you're not too badly affected by the experience. An instant after entering the glowing opening, you step out into an entirely different area.

Your new surroundings remind you of a hospital ward — a white-walled, clinical room containing several dozen identical beds. At the foot of each hangs a small portable display screen. The beds show signs of use, but are currently empty.

The Doctor lifts the display screen from the nearest bed and reads from it.

'Trial SS923. Hypomelanomic male. Age 43. Grafting procedure undertaken 20/10/25. New skin accepted. Full epidermal enclosure attained 27/10/25. UVB impermeability confirmed at 100 per —'

He breaks off as sounds of activity reach you along the one corridor that leads from the deserted ward.

To investigate the corridor, go to 60.
To search for an alternative exit, go to 94.

The boy shrugs, and replaces the blue stuff. 'I'm Blip by the way. Nice to meet some other folk who ain't Shiners.'

'Aren't what?' asks the Doctor.

'Shiners. Silver eyes and funny skin. Mind you, they was normal before.'

'So what happened to them?'

'The Second Skin project. You know the massive problem with the ozone layer? Well, Skinthetic, the company that owns this place have made artificial skin that blocks out UV rays. You stick a patch on your chest, and it grows to cover your whole body.'

Blip points to his shock of white hair.

'UV's more dangerous for me 'cos I'm hypomelanomic. That's why my hair and skin are so pale. So they thought I'd make a good test case. Only I ran before they could patch me. All the other testers got turned into Shiners. They're okay for a day or two, then their eyes silver over, and they start acting like zombies. The first ones to turn forced all the others on board to be patched.'

The Doctor looks worried.

'Blip, do you think you could get hold of one of these patches? I'm going to see if we can run a few tests.'

To go with the Doctor, go to 33. To go with Blip, go to 75.

With a little sonic magic, the Doctor removes the grille, and the two of you clamber up into the service void above. It is cramped and dark, but there is just room for you to squirm forward slowly.

Before long, you see a shaft of light ahead — another grille. The duct widens slightly, allowing you to wriggle alongside the Doctor. You peer down through the grille together.

In the room below, you can see four unconscious men, each strapped to an operating table by arm and leg restraints. Their upper bodies are bared. You are struck by the fact that their skin appears normal — unlike that of the strange humanoids you recently encountered.

You watch as a robotic arm swings across the first man's body and applies a small translucent patch to his chest.

The Doctor gestures for you to keep moving. A few metres ahead, the ventilation duct branches into two.

To crawl along the left-hand duct, go to 48.
To branch right, go to 35.

73 You clamber up into the robo-loader's harness, and try out its controls. A lever on the right seems to control the machine's overall movement, while two more near your left-hand operate its massive manipulating arms.

You clomp clumsily after the Doctor, whose path to the Fat Lady has been blocked by a group of Shiners. As he sends the nearest one reeling with a blow from his robo-loader's powerful fist, you thrust one of your left-hand levers to the side, and catch another of the Shiners with a fierce robotic right hook.

But your luck doesn't hold. With a scything sweep of laser fire, one of the Shiners cuts through the legs of the Doctor's robo-loader. As it falls, it crashes sideways into your machine, sending you toppling to the floor, too.

As you and the Doctor struggle free of your wrecked machines, the remaining Shiners advance menacingly.

To stand and fight, go to 12. To hastily retreat, go to 24.

74 Before you can take the second gadget from the Doctor, the doors at the end of the chamber suddenly part, and you are swept out of them as the chamber evacuates — into the emptiness of space beyond.

You tumble away from the space station, weightless. As you try to breathe, you panic. There doesn't seem to be any air inside your helmet.

The Doctor is floating not far from you, still clutching the second device. He points it directly away from you, and is suddenly propelled rapidly in your direction. It is clearly some sort of hand-held thruster.

Colliding with you, the Doctor grabs the other gadget — a black-capped cylinder — from your hand. He slams it against a valve in your helmet, and air gushes in, to your great relief.

Clinging to you with one arm, the Doctor uses the thruster gadget to steer you back towards the space station. A maintenance grab-rail on its hull comes within reach. You clutch it gratefully, then use it to haul your way across towards a pair of access hatches.

To try the left-hand hatch, go to 27. To try the one on the right, go to 79.

You accompany Blip along a sequence of passageways, until you arrive at an entrance marked CLONING LAB 1.

'This is where they grow the patches,' whispers Blip. He cautiously leads you through the doorway.

You're in luck — the laboratory is deserted. But Blip, moving among the workstations, seems less than pleased.

'Where are the patches? There should be one in each incubator...'

Then his eyes fall on the large white pod at the centre of the lab. He hurries over to examine it.

'Cargo pod. Bet it's full of 'em. They must be packing 'em up to send somewhere. And it's locked, worst luck.'

As Blip busies himself trying to break into the cargo pod, you take a look around. A door at the other side of the lab opens onto a narrow corridor. You wonder if it leads to an area where there might be more patches.

To explore the corridor, go to 30. To stay with Blip, go to 41.

The anti-gravity monorail carrying the cargo pods runs a few metres below the platform you are standing on. A service gantry runs alongside it. Following the Doctor's lead, you lower your body over the platform's edge, then drop quietly onto the gantry.

'Right — let's see if we can put a spanner in the works,' whispers the Doctor. 'Or rather a screwdriver.'

Pulling out his sonic screwdriver, he approaches a panel in the underside of the monorail track. But as he attempts to run the sonic around the panel's seal, it throws off a shower of sparks. The Doctor curses.

'It's shielded! This isn't going to be as easy as I thought.'

To make matters worse, you hear footsteps on the platform just above you. A Shiner is patrolling the area.

To escape by jumping down onto one of the cargo pods floating below the monorail, go to 25. To move quietly along the service gantry to where a ladder leads down to the hangar floor, go to 66.

The Doctor unslings the device from his shoulder. It reminds you of a large power-tool. A cluster of six needle-tipped darts are clipped to its side.

'This, my friend, is my antidote to our little skin problem. It's a bolt-gun from the Maintenance area — with a few small modifications.'

He unclips one of the darts and slots it into a narrow chamber in the top of the device. There's a clunk and hiss as the loading mechanism manoeuvres the dart into firing position.

'Each dart carries a charge of neurotoxin that targets non-human cells — the layer of alien tissue encasing each Shiner. Hit them with one of these, and you'll take out the exo-parasite for good. The sudden rebooting of the human host's nervous system will knock them out cold, but they'll come round just fine. Here you go.'

He hands the device to you with a smile.

'Just remember, you've only got six charges. Right — let's go!'

He steps forward into the Zoob, and you follow. An instant later you emerge into a huge open chamber. Directly ahead of you squats the colossal bulk of the Fat Lady, a giant orbital freighter. All around her, Shiners and service drones are busy with pre-launch preparations.

At the far side of the hangar, a pair of massive doors are slowly beginning to rumble open, revealing the blackness of space beyond.

Even as you take in the scene, you notice one of the Shiners striding in your direction, laser-pistol in hand, patrolling the hangar's perimeter.

To use your antidote gun, go to 10. To duck behind the nearby stack of containers, go to 84.

78 You dig the elbow of your free arm hard into your captor's abdomen. As he doubles over, you prepare to tackle his silver-eyed associate.

But there's no need. A small white-haired figure suddenly charges wildly into the second Shiner's side, knocking him to the ground. Blip has joined the fight.

'Let's get out of here!'

Before the Shiners can regain their feet, you and Blip sprint away. Neither of you knows where you're headed — only that you must get away, and fast.

Your flight takes you into a high-ceilinged area packed with machinery — some sort of processing plant. Blip pulls you down behind a large boiler-like vessel, and signals for you to be quiet.

Seconds later, the two Shiners burst through the entrance. As they begin to prowl among the machinery, Blip silently gestures to where a Zoob opening glows in the wall, not many metres away.

To try to reach the Zoob unnoticed, go to 11. To stay hidden, go to 69.

The hatch hisses open, and you clamber into the airlock chamber beyond. The Doctor seals the hatch, then activates the re-pressurisation controls. As he removes his helmet, you follow suit.

'Right — let's see where our unexpected little outing has brought us...'

The Doctor moves to the other end of the chamber and hits the door release. You emerge into a brightly-lit area, filled with a low, thrumming noise. The sound comes from an enormous transparent hemisphere, like a giant paperweight, that occupies the centre of the floor.

'Reactor,' says the Doctor. 'Must be the station's main power plant.'

Even as you take in your new surroundings, a zoom entrance flares into life in the wall nearby. Three silver-eyed figures step from it and stride towards you.

The Doctor braces his back against the wall and levels the hand-held thruster device at the approaching humanoids. As he squeezes the trigger, all three are sent sprawling backwards across the floor.

To try to continue holding off your attackers with the thruster, go to 7. To make a break for the Zoob while they recover, go to 87.

You're instantly returned to the place with three Zoob openings. Concerned that the Shiners may follow, you stagger into the left-hand Zoob, and are once more transported to a new location.

The experience of three Zoob journeys in quick succession has left you reeling. As you take a moment to let your insides settle down, your fears are realised — someone else steps from the Zoob. But it's only Blip.

'I thought you was with the Doctor?'

You explain about the ambush outside the TARDIS. Blip frowns.

'You never know — he might have got away. Strikes me he's pretty good at taking care of himself. If they did get him, they'll have taken him to the grafting theatres. That's where I was heading anyway — to grab a patch. Come on!'

You hurry after him, until he halts at a T-junction.

'Pretty certain the theatres are along one of these. But I can't remember which…'

To split up to search both corridors, go to 64. To stick together, go to 19.

The Doctor smiles.

'It might sound loopy to you, but trust me — it's the future out there!'

He hurries to the door and flings it open.

'See for yourself!'

As you step out, you catch your breath. The TARDIS is now standing in a large circular room. Its walls, floor and ceiling are predominantly transparent. Through them, you can see the star-speckled blackness of deep space.

You can also see the rest of the vast structure of which the bubble-like room is part. It is a space station, made up of a pair of giant hexagonal rings. Each ring comprises six large spheres, linked by cylindrical connecting arms. You are clearly viewing the space station from within one of its twelve apex spheres.

'Some sort of earth-orbiting facility,' says the Doctor. 'Commercial, I'd guess. That looks like a company name.' He points to a bold red logo — SKINTHETIC — on the side of one of the tubular connectors.

He turns his attention to your immediate surroundings.

'This must be an observation lounge. Oooh — look!'

In one of the few non-transparent sections of wall, there is a circular opening, filled with orange light. The Doctor strides eagerly towards it. Before you can ask what it is, the Doctor steps forward into its fluorescence, and vanishes.

To follow the Doctor into the peculiar opening, go to 49. To wait for him to return, go to 86.

As you try to move, you are surprised by someone's urgent whisper.

'Keep still! I've nearly got them off!'

It's Blip. He is concealed beneath the low belly of the Fat Lady right behind you, and is busily trying to prise your wrist restraints open with a small metal rod. Moments later, you feel your hands come free.

Your Shiner guards still have their backs to you. Seizing your chance, you slip silently under the spaceship to join Blip, and the two of you quickly slither away. You wriggle right the way across the Fat Lady's broad underside and emerge cautiously — only to find the other side of the hangar similarly bustling with Shiners and service drones.

'We could hide in the back of that hover-cart,' whispers Blip, pointing to a small vehicle hovering unattended nearby.

To lie low for a while, as Blip suggests, go to 50. To attempt to use the hover-cart to go to the doctor's aid, go to 88.

You run along one corridor after another, unable to shake off your pursuer. Then your luck runs out altogether. A pair of heavy doors seal the way ahead. As the Doctor hurriedly sets to work on them with his sonic screwdriver, the silver-eyed humanoid lumbers towards you.

'Got it!'

You dive through the opening doors. An instant later they slice decisively shut behind you, and you hear your pursuer's body slam against them.

'Ah...'

The Doctor is looking around with obvious alarm. You've entered a small chamber, at the far end of which is another set of heavy doors. Clamped to its walls are a row of bubble helmets and an assortment of hand-held gadgets.

'AIRLOCK ACTIVATED. DECOMPRESSION COMMENCING.'

The Doctor tears two helmets from the wall and tosses one to you.

'Put it on! Quickly!'

As you oblige, he grabs two of the hand-held devices and thrusts them at you.

To take the gadget in the Doctor's left hand first, go to 15. To grab the one in his right hand, go to 74.

You flatten yourself against the side of a container and listen to the Shiner's approaching footsteps, heart thumping. The creature halts, only a few metres from where you are hiding, and scans from side to side with its silver eyes. Then, to your great relief, it continues on its patrol.

The Doctor lets out a long breath. He gestures to the massive launch doors, now almost halfway open.

'You see that bulky thing above the doors? That's their motor unit. If we could put that out of action before the doors have fully opened, the Fat Lady would be stuck where she is.'

He points to a narrow metal walkway that runs around the top of the hangar walls and crosses above the huge doors.

'Look — there's a ladder up to that service gantry. I'm going to see if I can get up there and take out the doors. Wait here.'

To do as the Doctor says, go to 90. To insist on going with him, go to 54.

85 You flatten your body against the pod, as laser fire fizzes past. Then suddenly something seizes you, and lifts you high into the air.

You've been plucked from the pod by the mechanical hand of a massive machine. It is over twice the height of a human, and is being operated by a service drone, strapped into a control capsule within the machine's body.

As the drone manipulates its control levers, the giant robo-loader stomps away from the Fat Lady — carrying you away from the Doctor.

Suddenly, a small white-haired figure breaks from cover just ahead of the striding mechanical monster. It's Blip. He's clutching a metal bar, which he launches at the robo-loader's robotic operator. As the bar penetrates its thin metal casing, the drone explodes in a shower of sparks. The giant hand clutching you releases its grip, and you drop to the hangar floor.

'You okay?' asks Blip, helping you to your feet. 'Come on — we need to get out of here!'

'But the Doctor...' you protest.

To find somewhere to lie low, go to 50.
To use the robo-loader to go to the Doctor's aid, go to 88.

86 Shortly after he vanishes into the glowing opening, the Doctor suddenly reappears, with his eyes now tightly shut. As he steps forward from the haze of light, he opens them, and gives you a broad grin.

'That's better! The outward trip left me reeling. I'd forgotten how much travelling by Zoob messes with your senses. Keep your eyes closed — that's the secret!'

You ask what a 'Zoob' is.

'Zoom Tube. It's a rapid acceleration/deceleration device used during this Earth period — human scientists haven't cracked teleportation yet. A Zoob moves you along a relatively short fixed path almost instantaneously. I guess its how these folk move from one apex location to another.'

He points to the glowing opening.

'This one took me to somewhere called Taurus Apex. Some sort of waste-processing site. Not a soul about.'

To ask the Doctor where he thinks everybody is, go to 36. To see if you have more luck exploring via the corridor, go to 60.

After the familiar momentary jolt, you stumble out of the Zoob into a small, circular auditorium. Its multiple tiers of white benching are empty. You and the Doctor settle wearily on the front row, grateful for a moment's pause.

Without warning, a 3-D video projection flickers into life before you — a hologram of a young woman in a white lab coat. She casts a welcoming smile around the empty auditorium, and begins speaking.

'On behalf of the Skinthetic Corporation, welcome to the Second Skin product presentation. Following the rapid decline of the Earth's protective ozone layer over the last two centuries, humankind has been left at the mercy of the sun's deadly ultraviolet rays. But Skinthetic have come up with the perfect solution.'

Behind the woman, a giant Second Skin logo spirals into view.

'By applying a Second Skin patch — a small piece of synthetic tissue, which rapidly regenerates to encapsulate the entire body in an ultra-thin but UV-proof layer — customers can protect themselves from the everyday threat of skin cancer with the minimum of fuss and expense.'

Before she can continue, the Doctor points his sonic screwdriver, and the image crackles out of life.

To ask the Doctor what he thinks about the Second Skin idea, go to 92. To exit the auditorium, go to 46.

Before you have a chance to act, the wail of a klaxon suddenly fills the air, and green lights begin to flash above each of the hangar's exits. The entire host of Shiners and service drones start to vacate the area around the Fat Lady, quickly moving off to the exits. Within less than a minute, the hangar is deserted. The exit doors seal simultaneously.

'We'd better shift, too,' says Blip urgently. 'She must be ready to go. If we're too close when her thrusters kick in, we'll be frazzled.'

You hurriedly take cover behind a large section of dented hull that has been left leaning against one hangar wall — the legacy of a recent repair. It includes a small transparent section. Through it, you witness the ignition of the Fat Lady's rocket engines. Even shielded as you are, you can feel the searing heat generated by the roaring thrusters.

The massive space-freighter moves slowly towards the open hangar doors. Suddenly, something drops from the belly of the craft, into the inferno beneath it — a small, blue bubble. You can just make out a familiar figure encapsulated within it. Blip has seen it, too.

'It's the Doctor!'

As the Fat Lady approaches the threshold of the hangar, the Doctor makes his way towards you through her fiery exhaust plumes. He is clutching his sonic screwdriver, which you guess is generating the protective force-field around him.

By the time he reaches you, the Fat Lady has cleared the hangar doors, and is easing into open space beyond. As you emerge from behind the hull section, the Doctor deactivates his force field, and gives you a broad grin.

'Well, that's that taken care of!'

'But she made it.' Blip, like you, is confused. 'The patches will reach Earth.'

'I think not.' replies the Doctor. 'I wasn't on board long, but long enough to make a few minor technical adjustments.'

He holds up a fist full of tangled wiring.

'Knocked out the hull coolant system. Without it, she won't be able to keep her temperature down as she re-enters Earth's atmosphere. She'll burn up. Bye-bye Second Skin patches.'

His expression becomes more serious.

'Which still leaves us the problem of our remaining silver-eyed friends up here in orbit. So, how about we get you two equipped with a couple more antidote devices, and do a little de-Shining?'

He lays a hand on Blip's shoulder.

'Once everyone's back to normal, I'll drop you home on Earth in the TARDIS, Blip. Maybe you could show me and my friend here around a little — take in a few twenty-third century sights, eh?'

You grin. That sounds like fun...

THE END

Your insides eventually settle down, and you feel fit to join the Doctor in investigating your new surroundings.

Your Zoob ride has brought you to a gigantic warehouse. Aisle upon aisle of towering racking stretch away across the area's vast floor-space. The shelves are stacked with containers of all shapes, colours and sizes.

'Looks like we found the main supply stores,' observes the Doctor. 'I wonder if they have biscuits…'

Many of the miscellaneous containers are labelled: MEDICAL SUPPLY PACK ME776; PROTHIUM FILTERS 10 x 100; ANTI-CONTAM GLOVES: MEDIUM. The stretch of racking nearest you is loaded with several hundred white drums marked NUTRIENT GEL: GRADE C: 100L.

The word 'nutrient', together with the Doctor's mention of biscuits, make you suddenly realise how hungry you are.

To search the warehouse area for edible supplies, go to 94. To ask the Doctor what he thinks all the 'nutrient gel' is for, go to 36.

You watch anxiously as the Doctor hurries towards the ladder. Before he's even halfway there, a bolt of red energy rips across his path, narrowly missing him. As the Doctor flattens himself against the floor, a second laser bolt fizzes over his head. He's been spotted by a Shiner patrolling this side of the hangar.

Without hesitation, you lift the Doctor's antidote device to your shoulder, take aim, and squeeze the trigger. The Shiner is some distance away — it's a long shot, in every sense. But to your surprise, the neurotoxin-charged dart finds its target, penetrating the Shiner's arm. He slumps instantly to the floor.

As the Doctor gets to his feet and hurries back to join you, you slot another dart into the device's loading chamber. It's clear your cover is now blown — a second Shiner is striding purposefully in your direction.

To run for it, go to 24. To try another shot with the antidote device, go to 10.

Blip suggests that you begin your search for information in Gemini Apex, the space station's centre of operations. He leads you to a place where numerous Zoobs line the walls of a circular room — a sort of Zoob interchange. As you follow him into a particular one, you are transported to a large room crowded with hi-tech equipment.

Blip immediately crosses to one of the system terminals.

'I'll try to find out where the patches are stored, so we can get hold of one.'

The Doctor, meanwhile, has already spotted something on a surveillance screen.

'That's the TARDIS.'

He reads off the location at the bottom of the screen.

'Libra Apex, Area 7… Think I can probably find my way there. You two see what you can dig up. I'm going to nip back to the old girl and grab a few bits and bobs.'

And he hurries away.

To stay with Blip, go to 65. To go with the Doctor, go to 33.

Before the Doctor can reply, another voice — a child's — answers your question.

'It's a nightmare! They're creating monsters!'

A young boy with pale skin and white hair hurries towards you, his pink-tinged eyes wide with fear. You guess he's around eight or nine years old.

'They wanted to give me a patch. I'm hypomelanomic — ain't got enough pigment in my skin, which means that sunlight's even more dangerous for me. Guess they thought I'd be a good test case. But I wouldn't let 'em do it. I did a runner.'

He looks pleased with himself.

'I've been hiding out since, and I've seen what's happened to the others they've tested patches on — the people who work here, and a few volunteers. They start out okay. But then their skin goes all shimmery, and their eyes turn silver. They end up acting strange, like they're not human any more. Shiners, I call 'em.'

'And what's your name, my friend?' asks the Doctor warmly.

'Blip.'

'Well, Blip, it think it's high time we had a good look at one of these patches. Do you reckon you could get hold of one for me? I'm going to pop back to the TARDIS and pick up some diagnostic kit. If we run a few tests, we might be able to find out what we're dealing with.'

To go with the Doctor, go to 11. To help Blip track down a patch, go to 52.

Ranged along the wall nearest to you are a number of translucent square panels, each displaying a glowing red palm-print.

The Doctor places his right palm against one of the panels experimentally. A circular opening, filled with dazzling light, suddenly appears in the wall, rapidly expanding until it is the size of a doorway.

'ZOOB 7B, FOR TRANSIT TO SCORPIO APEX, ACTIVATED.'

'Excellent!' beams the Doctor. 'I'd forgotten all about Zoobs. Haven't visited this time period for long while. This'll be fun!'

You ask what a 'Zoob' is.

'Zoom Tube. It's a primitive method of moving something fast along a short, fixed path. Teleportation is still several centuries off. For now, Zoobs are the best way to get around quickly.'

He taps the side of his nose secretively.

'Top tip — when you use a Zoob, keep your eyes tight shut. Otherwise it really messes with your insides. Now, which one shall we try?'

To choose the Zoob that the Doctor has just activated, go to 70. To try the original one, go to 42.

Before you can begin your search, chaos breaks loose. An ear-splitting alarm fills the air, and several robotic contraptions emerge in rapid succession from the Zoob through which you arrived.

The robots are of various shapes and sizes — a squat, three-wheeled one with a flailing nozzle reminds you of a vacuum cleaner; another has a culinary implement at the end of each of its multiple arms. As they advance, their miscellaneous tools and attachments whirr and snap menacingly.

'Service drones,' says the Doctor, as you back away. 'They must have been reprogrammed to tackle intruders. I wonder why security is such a high priority?'

He glances up at the high ceiling, then hastily withdraws his sonic screwdriver. Without hesitating, he launches it into the air — directly into one of the bright ceiling lights.

There is a loud bang as the light explodes in a shower of sparks. An instant later a neighbouring light blows, then another, then another. The chain of explosions creates a circular fracture around a section of the ceiling. Breaking away, it plummets to the floor, crushing the advancing robots beneath it.

The Doctor casually catches his falling sonic screwdriver, then peers through the rising cloud of dust.

'I think they were just the advance guard...'

Following his gaze, you make out a group of humanoid figures stepping from the Zoob.

To quickly find somewhere to hide, go to 62. To dash for a second Zoob opening you've spotted nearby, go to 3.

Step into a world of wonder and mystery with Sarah Jane and her gang in:

1. Invasion of the Bane
2. Revenge of the Slitheen
3. Eye of the Gorgon
4. Warriors of the Kudlak

And don't miss these other exciting adventures with the Doctor!

1. The Spaceship Graveyard
2. Alien Arena
3. The Time Crocodile
4. The Corinthian Project
5. The Crystal Snare
6. War of the Robots
7. Dark Planet
8. The Haunted Wagon Train
9. Lost Luggage
10. Second Skin
11. The Dragon King
12. The Horror of Howling Hill